Polar Star

For Felicity Thomas
S.G.

For Tom
J.B.

Published by
PEACHTREE PUBLISHERS, LTD.
494 Armour Circle NE
Atlanta, Georgia 30324

Text © 1997 by Sally Grindley
Illustrations © 1997 by John Butler

First published by Orchard Books in Great Britain, 1997.

Printed in Singapore

10 9 8 7 6 5 4 3 2 1
First Edition

Library of Congress Cataloging-in-Publication Data
Grindley, Sally.
    Polar Star / Sally Grindley ; illustrated by John Butler. —1st ed.
        p. cm.
    Summary: Follows a mother polar bear and her two cubs from their birth to
a dangerous encounter with a hungry male bear, describing how the mother
protects her offspring until they can fend for themselves.
    ISBN 1-56145-181-9
    1. Polar bear—Juvenile fiction. [1. Polar bear—Fiction. 2. Bears—Fiction.
3. Animals—Infancy—Fiction.] I. Butler, John, 1952-   ill. II. Title.
PZ10.3.G886Po   1998
[E]—dc21
                                                    97-52593
                                                        CIP
                                                        AC

Polar Star

Sally Grindley

Illustrated by John Butler

PEACHTREE
ATLANTA

Deep beneath the frozen Arctic snow, Polar Star stirred in the cozy den she had built to protect herself from the winter cold.

Her fur was thicker than it had ever been, and she was fat, ready to feed her cubs when they were born. She would not eat again until the spring.

Polar Star gave birth to Snowball and Snowflake. They were small as kittens, blind and helpless. They nuzzled their way through their mother's fur until they reached her milk and fed hungrily. Then they slept.

For three months Polar Star fed and nursed her cubs, and soon they grew as big as puppies.

Up above, the days were growing lighter and the winds were less harsh. The time had come to leave the den.

Polar Star broke through the walls and gazed at the sparkling white world before her. She hauled herself out into the freezing air and threw herself into the snow, rolling over and over, a joyful jumble of fur and legs.

Snowball and Snowflake watched spellbound from the den, blinking furiously in the bright sunlight and squealing.

They watched and waited. Then they stumbled outside, step by slippery step, following their mother.

As the days passed, they quickly became bundles of trouble as they clambered on top of Polar Star and wrestled with each other. Their favorite game was to climb a steep slope and toboggan down, slipping and sliding on their tummies.

But now it was time for Polar Star to find food for herself. She set out, venturing over land and onto the treacherous sea ice.

She wove her way across the frozen wilderness, keeping her cubs close by, and stopping only to feed them and to sleep.

Soon they were far from land. Polar Star left her cubs to play and ambled to the edge of the ice. Snowball and Snowflake watched as their mother gave a great shudder of joy and plunged beneath the waves.

Moments later she heaved herself out, shook herself dry, and sniffed her way across the ice in search of food.

At last she stopped by a large hole, sat, and waited. Her wait was rewarded when the head of a seal popped up through the hole. She acted quickly. One cuff of her giant paw sent the seal crashing against the ice, and Polar Star had her first meal in five months.

While Snowball watched his mother, Snowflake wandered over to the water's edge, unaware that danger was closing in fast. A huge male polar bear was striding toward her. He was hungry and would think nothing of snatching a cub for food.

Snowball saw the big male bear and ran, squealing, to his mother.
Polar Star turned in alarm. She saw the male bear and rose up
on her hind legs, growling a terrible growl.

The male bear hesitated for a second, then grabbed at Snowflake. Polar Star charged, but the male bear reared up onto his hind legs and struck her and struck her again. Polar Star fell backward. Then she hurled herself at the male bear again, pummelling him with her paws and roaring with fury.

At last the male bear backed away, shaken by her fearlessness, and began to lick his wounds.

Polar Star didn't waste any time. She gathered the terrified cubs to her and raced them away across the ice.

They walked for miles. At last darkness swept round them,
and Polar Star scoured the landscape for shelter.

She tunnelled into a mound of drifted snow and built a den. There, Snowball and Snowflake snuggled up tight in the folds of her enormous body and felt safe again.

The world outside was an exciting place, but it was full of danger. Polar Star would be there to protect her cubs until they were old enough and wise enough to look after themselves.

Polar Bear Facts

Polar bears survive in the freezing cold of the high Arctic, spending most of their time on pack ice far from land. Their thick white fur covers a layer of fat that keeps them warm. They are excellent swimmers and can spend hours in the icy waters.

They are the largest meat-eating land mammals. Polar bears feed mostly on seals, grabbing them when they come up for air at breathing holes in the ice. They may even kill small whales and walruses.

In November and December, pregnant female bears dig dens in the snow and disappear inside until the following March or April. During that time, they give birth to one, two, or sometimes three tiny cubs. The cubs feed on their mother's milk. When they are about three months old, the cubs leave the den with their mother. They stay with her until they are just over two years old.

The polar bear cubs' greatest enemies are hungry male polar bears, for whom they are an easy source of food. The only enemy that adult polar bears have is man.